HAROLD
the hairiest man

ORCHARD BOOKS
96 Leonard Street, London EC2A 4RH
Orchard Books Australia
14 Mars Road, Lane Cove, NSW 2066
Text © Laurence Anholt 1997
Illustrations © Tony Ross 1997
First published in Great Britain in 1997
First paperback publication 1998
The right of Laurence Anholt to be identified as the author
and Tony Ross and the illustrator of this work
has been asserted by them in accordance with the
Copyright, Designs and Patents Act, 1988.
A CIP catalogue record for this book is available
from the British Library.
1 86039 552 X (hardback)
1 86039 624 0 (paperback)
Printed in Great Britain

HAROLD
the hairiest man

Laurence Anholt
Illustrated by Tony Ross

ORCHARD BOOKS

We are going to meet Harold.
We are going to meet Harold, the
hairiest man in the WHOLE
UNIVERSE. Nobody is hairier
than Harold.

Harold is proud of the way he looks. Harold has a big mirror so that he can see all his beautiful hair.

Harold has a shelf covered with
brushes and combs and bottles of
shampoo.

Every morning, Harold stands in front of his big mirror and says, "Hello, Harold, you lovely big hairy man."

Then...
Harold brushes his big bushy
beard.

And Harold curls his twisty
moustache.

And Harold washes his beautiful
long hair.

It takes a very long time.
Because Harold has hairs in his
nose.

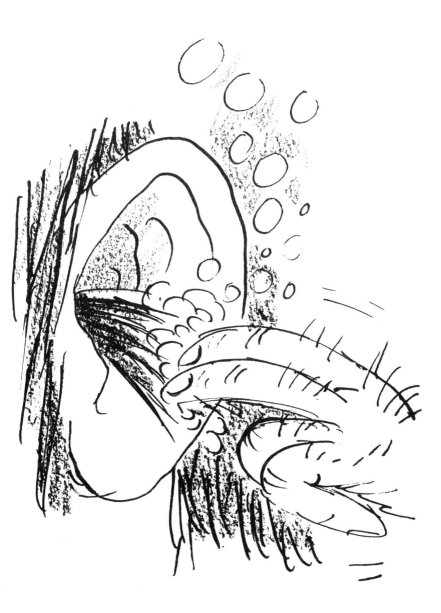

And Harold has hairs in his ears.

And Harold has huge eyebrows.

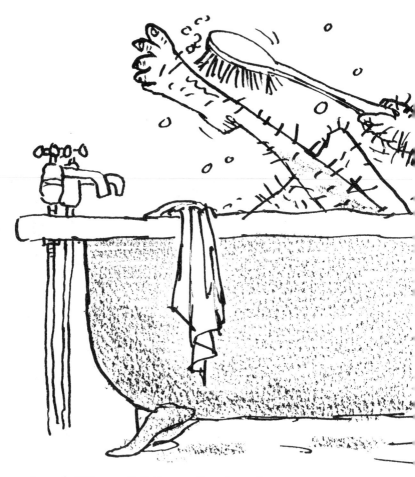

And Harold has hairy legs.

And Harold has hairy hands.

And Harold has hairs on his chest,
his knees, his neck, his nose.

Harold has hairs on his elbows,
his belly, his back, his toes.

One day, Harold went for a walk.
He walked past a shop. A
beautiful woman was working
inside.

"Hello, Harold, you lovely big hairy man," she called.

Harold and the woman fell
in love.
The woman was a famous
hairdresser. Her name was
Shirley.

Harold loved Shirley's shop
because it was full of big mirrors
and lots of combs and brushes.

Shirley loved Harold's hair. She
liked to practise all the latest
styles.

Everyone who passed the shop wanted Shirley to do their hair too. "We want beautiful hair just like Harold," they said.

Harold had a side parting.

Everyone wanted a side parting.

Harold had a centre parting.

Everyone wanted a centre parting.

Harold had his hair brushed back.

Everyone wanted their hair
brushed back.

Harold had his hair brushed
forward.

Everyone wanted their hair
brushed forward.

Harold had a spiky mohican.

Everyone wanted a spiky
mohican.

Harold and Shirley were very happy. They decided to get married and live together above Shirley's shop.

But Harold took so long getting
ready that he almost missed the
wedding.

He didn't want to go on
honeymoon. He thought the sun
would be bad for his hair and the
seaweed would get caught in his
beard.

Shirley began to get cross. She liked to go dancing in the evenings but Harold always had to stay in and wash his hair.

When Shirley saw Harold looking
in the mirror and saying, "Hello,
Harold, you lovely big hairy
man," she began to get jealous.

She thought that Harold must love his hair more than he loved her.

So Shirley did a terrible thing. The worst thing that anyone can do to a hairy man.

When Harold was asleep, she took
her hairdressing scissors and
snipped off his beautiful hair.

Then she chopped off Harold's
beard.

Then Shirley took her hairdresser's shaver and shaved Harold from head to foot until he was as smooth as a baby bunny's bottom.

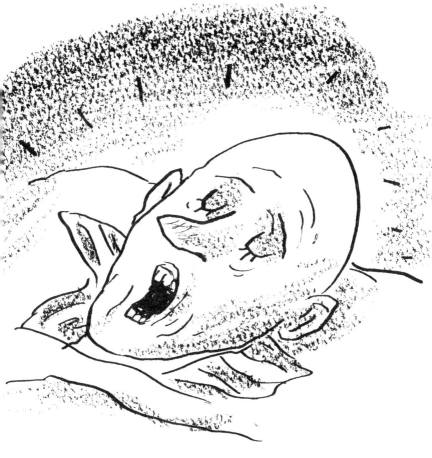

When Harold woke up he went to the mirror. He said, "Hello, Harold, you lovely big...AAARRRGGGH!"

Then Harold began to cry.
"Someone has stolen my beautiful
hair," he sobbed. "Someone has
stolen my beautiful hair."

Harold went downstairs to
Shirley's shop in his pyjamas.
Everybody stared at him.
Shirley went over to Harold and
kissed his bald head.

Then Harold began to cry.
"Someone has stolen my beautiful
hair," he sobbed. "Someone has
stolen my beautiful hair."

Harold went downstairs to
Shirley's shop in his pyjamas.
Everybody stared at him.
Shirley went over to Harold and
kissed his bald head.

Then everyone in the shop said,
"We want to be bald, too. Just like
Harold."

Harold looked at himself in all the mirrors. Then Harold began to smile. He stroked his smooth bald head.

"Hello, Harold, you lovely big bald man," he said.